# My Dentist, My Friend

## P. K. Hallinan

ideals children's books.
Nashville, Tennessee

ISBN 0-8249-5388-6

Published by Ideals Children's Books
An imprint of Ideals Publications
A division of Guideposts
535 Metroplex Drive, Suite 250
Nashville, Tennessee 37211
www.idealspublications.com

Printed and bound in Mexico by RR Donnelley & Sons.

**Library of Congress has already cataloged this book as follows:**
Hallinan, P.K.
     My dentist, my friend / written and illustrated by P.K. Hallinan.
          p.    cm.
     Summary: A visit to the dentist is shown to be nothing to fear.
     [1. Dentists—Fiction. 2. Dental Care—Fiction. 3. Teeth—Care and hygiene—Fiction. 4. Stories in
     rhyme.] I. Title.
     PZ8.3.H15My    1996
     [E]—dc20                                                    95-37592
                                                    CIP
                                                    AC

For Lin Mattson, whose friendship has never needed a filling.

# Books by P. K. Hallinan

A Rainbow of Friends

For the Love of Our Earth

Heartprints

How Do I Love You?

I'm Thankful Each Day!

Just Open a Book

Let's Learn All We Can!

My Dentist, My Friend

My Doctor, My Friend

My First Day of School

My Teacher's My Friend

That's What a Friend Is

Today Is Christmas!

Today Is Easter!

Today Is Halloween!

Today Is Thanksgiving!

Today Is Valentine's Day!

Today Is Your Birthday!

We're Very Good Friends, My Brother and I

We're Very Good Friends, My Father and I

We're Very Good Friends, My Grandma and I

We're Very Good Friends, My Grandpa and I

We're Very Good Friends, My Mother and I

We're Very Good Friends, My Sister and I

When I Grow Up

10 8 6 4 2 1 3 5 7 9

My dentist, my friend—
what more can I say?
My dentist has helped me
to smile this way!

Yes, dentists are helpful
in all that they do.
They keep our teeth clean—
and healthier too!

When we go to the dentist,
we usually will find
a lobby that's hopping
with sights of all kinds.

There are children with toys.
There are parents with books.
There are dental assistants
with welcoming looks.

And music plays lazily
filling the halls
as everyone waits
for their name to be called.

The next thing we know. . .
we're ready to go!

The oral hygienist shows kindness and care as we're led to a room with a big, comfy chair.

We hop right on up,
with a bib 'round our neck,
and a very bright light
inspects every speck.

First, a peek to the north. . .
Then, a peek to the south. . .
The hygienist peruses
each tooth in our mouth.

The cleaning begins,
and there's plenty to do.
Our plaque is removed. . .
and our tartar is too!

Then each tooth turns white
and remarkably bright!

At last comes the dentist,
when the cleaning is through,
for a gentle exam
and a thoughtful review.

The dentist is thorough
and takes a long look—
inspecting for cavities
and checking each nook.

We might need some x-rays,
but that's kind of fun.
We wear a lead apron,
and suddenly—we're done!

Our checkup, we're told,
is better than gold!

We're given a toothbrush,
some floss, and some praise,
'cause regular brushing
kept cavities away.

And they send us along
with a ten-gallon smile
that's good for six months—
well, at least for a while.

Yes, dentists *are* helpful—
there's really no doubt.
Their care and concern
are what friendship's about.

So, I guess there's no question
why I trust and depend
on this *special* person. . .

my dentist, my friend!